# The Fabulous *Flying Flag* Farm

BY

Nancy Robinson Masters

ILLUSTRATED BY

Debra H. Warr

The Fabulous Flying Flag Farm


MasAir Publications
MasAir, Inc.
4918 Newman Road
Abilene, Texas 79601

Manufactured in Abilene, Texas by Quality Printing Company

Produced by John R. Matthews, Inc.

An Ups and Downs Book

ISBN 0-9623563-5-2

*This book is for all those who made it possible for us to pledge allegiance to the Flag of the United States of America.*

*NRM DHW*

"Here she comes!" a cowboy hollered.

The rider on the white horse led the 4th of July Parade down Swenson Avenue.

She carried the flag of the United States of America!

Everyone clapped and cheered.

Everyone except me, Nancy Robinson.

I stood very straight with my hand over my heart. That was what Mama taught me to do when the flag passes by.

"Our flag is *fabulous*!" Mama said.

"It belongs to every citizen of the United States of America."

Clippety, clippety, clippety-clop!

The white horse trotted closer. The Stars and Stripes waved proudly in the summer breeze.

I wished *I* could be the girl who carried the flag.

"When we say the Pledge of Allegiance to the Flag we are making a promise," Mama said.

"A promise to work together for our country, no matter how different each of us may be."

Ed Roy Odom was different.

He kept squirmy things in his notebook. He put ketchup on everything he ate — even ice cream. He thought girls were dumb.

Each time we said the Pledge of Allegiance to the Flag last year in school, Ed Roy would have the hiccups.

On purpose.

I looked to see if Ed Roy was at the parade.

There were people sitting on the sidewalk. There were people listening to radios. There were lots of cowboys wearing big, tall hats.

I did not see Ed Roy.

The white horse stopped in front of me. The band played "The Star-Spangled Banner." The band finished playing the national anthem.

"I pledge allegiance to the flag of the United States of America, and to the Republic for which it stands, one Nation under God, indivisible, with liberty and justice for all."

Oh, man!

The people sitting on the sidewalk... just kept sitting.

The people listening to the radio... just kept listening.

Only the cowboys took their hats off as Old Glory passed by.

"Hic!"

Ed Roy was standing behind me eating an ice cream cone. He had ketchup all over his face.

"Dumb girl!" he yelled, sticking a squirmy thing on my back. Then he ran.

Oh, man.

Maybe Mama was wrong about our flag being fabulous.

"How do you grow flags?" I asked Mama that afternoon. She was working in the garden behind the barn.

"Well, first you get some flower bulbs. Then you—"

"*Flags*, Mama. Not flowers. I want to grow *flags*. Red, white and blue ones with stars."

"Did you say you want to grow flags?" Dad's voice boomed from the barn.

"The very best flags are made from cotton. The only way flags will grow is to hoe. Come with me to the field and I'll show you."

He handed me a hoe with a sharp, shiny blade. Then he showed me the difference between the cotton plants and the weeds.

Chop! Chop! Chop!

Down went the weeds.

We walked the long rows of cotton hoeing every weed we found.

"Where are the flags?" I asked.

"Just keep hoeing and flags will grow," Dad said.

"How long will it take?"

"The cotton we grow on our farm has to be made into cloth. The cloth will be made into flags. That's how flags grow," Dad explained.

He was *so* proud to be a farmer.

"It takes many different people working together to make our flag. Just like it has taken many different people working together to make our country."

I went to the field to hoe cotton with Dad every morning. He told me about all the places the Star-Spangled Banner flies: places like our Capitol in Washington, D.C.; places like a tiny island called Iwo Jima; places like the South Pole, at the very bottom of the world!

One morning an airplane circled over us.

"I want to be a pilot when I grow up and fly to all those places," I told Dad. I was getting tired of hoeing.

"If you hoe, there is no telling how far you will go," Dad promised.

The first day back in school, Miss Parker made an announcement to our class.

"We are each going to grow something different for the Harvest Festival in November. You may choose what you want to grow."

Ed Roy's hand shot up first.

"Tomatoes!" he said. He still had ketchup on his fingers from eating french fries.

"Peanuts!" said Hubie Hernandez. Hubie's mama made muy bueno peanut butter sandwiches.

"Sweet potatoes," said Alice Abernathy.

Oh, man.

I wanted to grow sweet potatoes. Now I had to think of something else.

"I will grow flags," I said. "*American* flags."

All the kids in Miss Parker's room laughed.

"Nancy is very patriotic," Miss Parker said.

The kids stopped laughing when she wrote "FLAGS" in big letters by my name on the board.

"What's *patriotic*?" Ed Roy asked Hubie when Miss Parker wasn't looking.

"It's loving our country more than you love ketchup."

When Hubie said that, Ed Roy shook his head. There was *nothing* he loved better than ketchup.

He threw a squirmy thing on my desk.

"You can't grow flags. Girls are so dumb."

Then he laughed himself into a great big hiccup.

"My dad says if you hoe, flags will grow," I insisted, and threw the squirmy thing back at him.

By November, I wasn't so sure.

The Harvest Festival was only five days away. Ed Roy's tomato plant was almost as big as he was.

There were ten tiny peanuts on Hubie's goober vine.

Alice's sweet potato had sprouted so many roots it looked like my cat's whiskers.

I was the only kid in Miss Parker's room who didn't have something to show. It had not rained on our farm all summer. Hardly any puffs of cotton were on the stalks.

"Where is Nancy's *hoe*-made flag?" Ed Roy asked every morning when we said the Pledge of Allegiance.

Oh, man.

I wished I had never told Miss Parker and the kids about hoeing cotton with Dad all summer. I wished I had never said I could grow flags. I wished I could stop having the hiccups.

Maybe Ed Roy was right. Maybe girls were dumb.

The morning of the Harvest Festival Miss Parker was not at school. I was glad. I did not want her to know my flags didn't grow.

Mr. Fu, the principal, came to our room just before it was time to go to lunch.

"We are going on a field trip. Hubie Hernandez' mama made peanut butter sandwich sack lunches for everyone! We are going to Nancy Robinson's fabulous flying flag farm to see how flags grow."

*OH, NO!*

All the kids in Miss Parker's class clapped and cheered. All the kids except me and Ed Roy. *He* did not want to miss having tomato pizza for lunch in the cafeteria.

*I* did not want the kids to see my stalks of dried-up cotton.

Hic! Hic! Hic!

The school bus bumped and thumped to a stop by our farm. This is the worst day of my whole life, I thought. My stomach felt like it was stuck together with peanut butter.

Wait a minute. There was Miss Parker!

"Hooray for the Red, White and Blue!" she told the kids as they got off the bus.

"Look!"

Oh, man!

It was my dad. He was dressed to look like Uncle Sam! He was standing in the cotton field...

AND THE COTTON FIELD WAS FULL OF
FABULOUS FLYING
FLAGS!

"Muy bueno!" Hubie yelled.

"How sweet!" Alice squealed.

"Hic!" was all Ed Roy could say. His eyes were as big as tomatoes.

Miss Parker was laughing hard. She and Mama and Dad had spent all morning sticking those flagpoles into the soft dirt by the cotton stalks to surprise us!

Dad showed Hubie the difference between cotton plants and weeds. He showed Alice how to hoe. He let each kid pick one of the flags to take back to school. He even let Ed Roy pick the *biggest* flag in our field.

"Here she comes!" Ed Roy Odom hollered.

He was standing very straight with his hand over his heart.

"I pledge allegiance to the flag of the United States of America, and to the Republic for which it stands, one Nation under God, indivisible, with liberty and justice for all."

Ed Roy said the Pledge of Allegiance to the Flag without a single hiccup.

Everyone clapped and cheered as the kids in Miss Parker's room led the Harvest Festival parade.

Everyone except me, Nancy Robinson.

I CARRIED THE FLAG!

## Let's show Ed Roy Odom the correct way to say the Pledge of Allegiance to the Flag of the United States of America.

Stand very straight facing the flag. Place your right hand over your heart. Men and boys should remove their hats (unless in military uniform.)

Say the words slowly. Think about each word as you say,

I pledge allegiance
to the flag
of the United States of America,
and to the Republic
for which it stands,
one Nation under God, indivisible,
with liberty and justice for all.

**What should Ed Roy do when the national anthem is played?**

Even if there is not a flag present, do everything exactly the same as you would do when you say the Pledge of Allegiance.

**What are some other ways Ed Roy can show respect to the flag?**

Never dip the flag to any person or thing.

Never let the flag touch anything beneath it, such as the ground or the floor.

Never permit the flag to be damaged in any way.

**Flag Facts**

Ed Roy knows...

There are thirteen stripes on the flag. Seven are red, six are white.

There are 50 stars on the blue field. One for each state in the United States of America.

The original Pledge of Allegiance to the Flag was written by Francis Bellamy in 1892.

The Pledge of Allegiance as we say it today was recognized by an Act of Congress in 1954.

Each year on June 14 we celebrate Flag Day, the birthday of our flag.

**Can you help Ed Roy find these nicknames for the flag in *THE FABULOUS FLYING FLAG FARM*?**

Old Glory

Stars and Stripes

Star-Spangled Banner

The Red, White and Blue

An Ups and Downs Book